W9-BCP-668

Granfa' Grig Had a Pig

and Other Rhymes Without Reason from Mother Goose

398
Mot

Granfa' Grig Had a Pig

and Other Rhymes Without Reason from Mother Goose

Compiled and Illustrated
by Wallace Tripp

Little, Brown and Company

Boston   Toronto

CROOKED CREEK SCHOOL LIBRARY
MSD WASHINGTON TOWNSHIP
INDIANAPOLIS, INDIANA

ILLUSTRATIONS COPYRIGHT © 1976 BY WALLACE TRIPP

ALL RIGHTS RESERVED. NO PART OF THIS BOOK MAY BE REPRODUCED IN ANY FORM
OR BY ANY ELECTRONIC OR MECHANICAL MEANS INCLUDING INFORMATION STORAGE
AND RETRIEVAL SYSTEMS WITHOUT PERMISSION IN WRITING FROM THE PUBLISHER,
EXCEPT BY A REVIEWER WHO MAY QUOTE BRIEF PASSAGES IN A REVIEW.

FIRST EDITION

T 11/76

The following appear in this collection by permission of the Oxford
University Press: four rhymes from *The Oxford Dictionary of Nursery
Rhymes* edited by Iona and Peter Opie (1951); two from *The Oxford
Nursery Rhyme Book* assembled by Iona and Peter Opie (1955); two
from *The Puffin Book of Nursery Rhymes* © Iona and Peter Opie
(1963).

Library of Congress Cataloging in Publication Data

Mother Goose.
    Granfa' Grig had a pig, and other rhymes without reason.

    SUMMARY: A selection of Mother Goose rhymes including
"Old King Cole," "Jack Be Nimble," and many other well-
and lesser-known verses.
    1. Nursery rhymes. [1. Nursery rhymes] I. Tripp,
Wallace. II. Title.
PZ8.3.M85Tr   398.8   [398.8]   76-25234
ISBN 0-316-85282-1
ISBN 0-316-85284-8 pbk.

*Published simultaneously in Canada
by Little, Brown & Company (Canada) Limited*

PRINTED IN THE UNITED STATES OF AMERICA

Fee, Fie, Fo, Fum!
I smell the blood of an Englishman.
Be he alive or be he dead,
I'll grind his bones to make my bread.

If I'd as much money as I could spend,
I never would cry old chairs to mend;
Old chairs to mend, old chairs to mend,
I never would cry old chairs to mend;

If I'd as much money as I could tell,
I never would cry old clothes to sell;
Old clothes to sell, old clothes to sell,
I never would cry old clothes to sell.

Jeanie come tie my,
Jeanie come tie my,
Jeanie come tie my bonnie cravat;
I've tied it behind,
I've tied it before,
And I've tied it so often, I'll tie it no more.

I'm the king of the castle,
Get you down you dirty rascal.

Pussy cat, pussy cat, where have you been?
I've been to London to visit the Queen.
Pussy cat, pussy cat, what did you there?
I frightened a little mouse under her chair.

Tommy kept a chandler's shop,
Richard went to buy a mop,
Tommy gave him such a knock,
That sent him out of his chandler's shop.

Millery, millery, dustipoll,
How many sacks have you stole?
Four and twenty and a peck:
Hang the miller up by his neck!

What's the news of the day,
Good neighbor, I pray?
They say the balloon
Has gone up to the moon!

I had a little dog, and his name was Blue Bell,
I gave him some work, and he did it very well;
I sent him upstairs to pick up a pin,
He stepped into the coal-scuttle up to the chin.
I sent him to the garden to pick some sage,
He tumbled down and fell in a rage;
I sent him to the cellar, to draw a pot of beer,
He came up again and said there was none there.

There was a crooked man, and he went a crooked mile,
He found a crooked sixpence against a crooked stile;
He bought a crooked cat, which caught a crooked mouse,

And they all lived together in a little crooked house.

The grand old Duke of York,
He had ten thousand men;
He marched them up to the top of the hill,
And he marched them down again.
And when they were up, they were up,
And when they were down, they were down,
And when they were only half-way up,
They were neither up nor down.

One thing at a time
And that done well,
Is a very good rule,
As many can tell.

Doctor Foster went to Glo'ster
In a shower of rain.
He stepped in a puddle,
Right up to his middle,
And never went there again.

There was an old woman lived under the hill,
And if she's not gone she lives there still.
Baked apples she sold, and cranberry pies,
And she's the old woman that never told lies.

MIGHT BE A FEW WORMS IN THOSE APPLES, SIR. POOR CRANBERRIES THIS YEAR. MAY BE TOO MUCH SALT IN ....

Dingty diddledy,
My mammy's maid,
She stole oranges,
I am afraid;
Some in her pocket,
Some in her sleeve,
She stole oranges,
I do believe.

Bat, bat, come under my hat,
And I will give you a slice of bacon,
And when I bake,
I'll give you a cake,
If I am not mistaken.

Of a little take a little,
Manners so to do;
Of a little leave a little,
That is manners, too.

Peter White will ne'er go right,
Would you know the reason why?
He follows his nose wherever he goes,
And that stands all awry.

Old King Cole was a merry old soul,
And a merry old soul was he;
He called for his pipe,
And he called for his bowl,
And he called for his fiddlers three.

Each fiddler he had a fiddle,
And the fiddles went tweedle-dee;
Oh, there's none so rare as can compare
With King Cole and his fiddlers three.

Then he called for his fifers two,
And they puffed and they blew tootle-oo;
And King Cole laughed as his glass he quaffed,
And his fifers puffed tootle-oo.

Then he called for his drummer boy,
The army's pride and joy,
And the thuds out-rang with a loud bang! bang!
The noise of the noisiest toy.

BULLY!

BANG!
BANG!

Then he called for his trumpeters four,
Who stood at his own palace door,
And they played trang-a-tang
Whilst the drummer went bang,
And King Cole he called for more.

TRANG-A-TANG

He called for a man to conduct,
Who into his bed had been tuck'd,
And he had to get up without bite or sup
And waggle his stick and conduct.

Old King Cole laughed with glee,
Such rare antics to see;
There never was a man in merry England
Who was half as merry as he.

An apple a day
Keeps the doctor away.

There was an old woman
Lived under the hill,
She put a mouse in a bag,
And sent it to the mill;

The miller did swear,
By the point of his knife,
He never took toll
Of a mouse in his life!

Hickory, dickory, dock,
The mouse ran up the clock.
The clock struck one,
And down he run,
Hickory, dickory, dock.

A wise old owl lived in an oak;
The more he saw the less he spoke;
The less he spoke the more he heard.
Why aren't we all like that wise old bird?

Four stiff-standers,
Four dilly-danders,
Two lookers, two crookers,
And a wig-wag.

Two brothers we are, great burdens we bear,
On which we are bitterly pressed;
The truth is to say, we are full all the day,
And empty when we go to rest.

On London bridge what made me start
Was fingers and thumbs all heaped in a cart.

See, see! What shall I see?
A horse's head where his tail should be.

Two legs sat upon three legs
With one leg in his lap;
In comes four legs
And runs away with one leg.
Up jumps two legs,
Catches up three legs,
Throws it after four legs,
And makes him bring back one leg.

27

Gray goose and gander,
Waft your wings together,
And carry the good king's daughter
Over the one-strand river.

Little Miss Muffet
Sat on a tuffet,
Eating her curds and whey;
There came a big spider,
Who sat down beside her
And frightened Miss Muffet away.

The little priest of Felton,
The little priest of Felton,
He killed a mouse within his house,
And no one there to help him.

Slug-a-bed,
Slug-a-bed,
Barley butt,
Your bum is so heavy
You can't get up.

Humpty Dumpty sat on a wall,
Humpty Dumpty had a great fall.
All the king's horses
And all the king's men,
Couldn't put Humpty together again.

There was a mad man and he had a mad wife,
And they lived in a mad town;
They had three children all at a birth,
And mad they were every one.

The father was mad, the mother was mad,
And the children mad beside;
And they all got on a mad horse,
And madly they did ride.

They rode by night and they rode by day,
Yet never a one of them fell;
They rode so madly all the way,
Till they came to the gates of hell.

Old Nick was glad to see them so mad,
And gladly let them in :
But he soon grew sorry to see them so merry,
And let them out again.

A hedge between,
Keeps friendship green.

Higgleby, piggleby, my black hen,
She lays eggs for gentlemen;
Sometimes nine, and sometimes ten,
Higgleby, piggleby, my black hen!

Wear you a hat or wear you a crown,
All that goes up, must surely come down.

As I was going to Darby,
Upon a market day,
I met the biggest ram, sir,
That ever was fed on hay.

This ram was fat behind, sir,
This ram was fat before,
This ram was ten yards high, sir,
Indeed he was no more.

The wool upon his back, sir,
It reached unto the sky,
The eagles built their nest there,
For I heard the young ones cry.

The wool on this ram's belly, sir,
Went dragging to the ground.
The Devil cut it off, sir,
To make himself a gown.

The horns on this ram's head, sir,
They reached up to the moon,
A man went up them in March, sir,
And never came down till June.

The space between the horns, sir,
Was as far as a man could reach,
And there they built a pulpit,
But no one in it preached.

He had four feet to walk, sir,
He had four feet to stand,
And every foot he had, sir,
It covered an acre of land.

And one of this ram's teeth, sir,
Was hollow as a horn,
And when they took its measure, sir,
It held a bushel of corn.

Now the man who fed this ram, sir,
He fed him twice a day,
And each time that he fed him, sir,
He ate a rick of hay.

The wool upon his tail, sir,
Was very fine and thin,
Took all the girls in Darby town
Full seven years to spin.

The man that owned this ram, sir,
He was so very rich;
And the man that made this song, sir,
He died last year with the itch.

Indeed, sir, it's the truth, sir,
For I never was taught to lie,
And if you go to Darby, sir,
You may eat a bit of the pie.

A little old man of Derby,
How do you think he served me?
He took away my bread and cheese,
And that is how he served me.

Peter, Peter, pumpkin-eater,
Had a wife and couldn't keep her;
He put her in a pumpkin shell,
And there he kept her very well.

Richard Dick upon a stick,
Sandy on a sow,
We'll ride away to Colley Fair
To buy a horse to plow.

My nose is green,
Yours is blue;
Sister has got a red one,
What's that to you?

Different people have different 'pinions,
Some like apples and some like inions.

Old woman, old woman,
Shall we go a-shearing?
Speak a little louder, sir,
I am very thick of hearing.
Old woman, old woman,
Shall I love you dearly?
Thank you, kind sir,
I hear you very clearly.

Wooley Foster had a cow,
Black and white about the brow;
Open the gate and let her through,
Wooley Foster's old cow!

There were three jovial huntsmen,
As I have heard men say,
And they would go a-hunting
Upon St. David's Day.

All the day they hunted
And nothing could they find,
But a ship a-sailing,
A-sailing with the wind.

One said it was a ship,
The other he said, Nay;
The third said it was a house,
With the chimney blown away.

And all the night they hunted
And nothing could they find,
But the moon a-gliding,
A-gliding with the wind.

One said it was the moon,
The other he said, Nay;
The third said it was a cheese,
And half of it cut away.

And all day they hunted
And nothing could they find,
But a hedgehog in a bramble bush,
And that they left behind.

The first said it was a hedgehog,
The second he said, Nay;
The third said it was a pincushion,
And the pins stuck in wrong way.

And all the night they hunted
And nothing could they find,
But a hare in a turnip field,
And that they left behind.

The first said it was a hare,
The second he said, Nay;
The third said it was a calf,
And the cow had run away.

And all the day they hunted
And nothing could they find,
But an owl in a holly tree,
And that they left behind.

One said it was an owl,
The other he said, Nay;
The third said it was the evil one,
And they all ran away.

43

Here I am, little jumping Joan;
When nobody's with me,
I'm all alone.

Old Mistress McShuttle
Lived in a coal-scuttle,
Along with her dog and her cat;
What they ate I can't tell,
But 'tis known very well,
That none of the party were fat.

Old Mistress McShuttle
Scoured out her coal-scuttle,
And washed both her dog and her cat;
The cat scratched her nose,
So they came to hard blows,
And who was the gainer by that?

The man in the wilderness asked me,
How many strawberries grew in the sea?
I answered him, as I thought good,
As many as red herring grew in the wood.

William and Mary, George and Anne,
Four such children had never a man!
They put their father to flight and shame,
And called their brother a shocking bad name.

Little Shon a Morgan,
Gentleman of Wales,
Came riding on a nanny goat,
Selling of pig's tails.

Taffy was born
On a moon shiny night,
His head in the pipkin,
His heels upright.

A knight of Cales, a gentleman of Wales,
And a laird of the north countree;
A yeoman of Kent with his yearly rent
Will buy them out all three.

Higglety, pigglety, pop!
The dog has eaten the mop;
The pig's in a hurry,
The cat's in a flurry,
Higglety, pigglety, pop!

As I went to Bonner,
I met a pig
Without a wig,
Upon my word and honor.

Who comes here?
   A grenadier.
What do you want?
   A pot of beer.
Where's your money?
   I've forgot.
Get you gone,
   You drunken sot!

Diddle, diddle, dumpling, my son John,
Went to bed with his trousers on;
One shoe off, and one shoe on,
Diddle, diddle, dumpling, my son John.

When the sun's perpendicular height
Points out the depths of the sea,
And when the fishes in the water sweat,
Oh my, how hot it will be!

Ugly babies
Make pretty ladies.

When I was a little boy, my mother kept me in,
Now I am a big boy, and fit to serve the king;
I can handle a musket, I can smoke a pipe,
I can kiss a pretty girl at ten o'clock at night.

Round about, round about,
Gooseberry-pie,
My father loves good ale,
And so do I.

Arthur O'Bower has broken his band
And he comes roaring up the land;
The King of Scots with all his power
Cannot stop Arthur of the Bower.

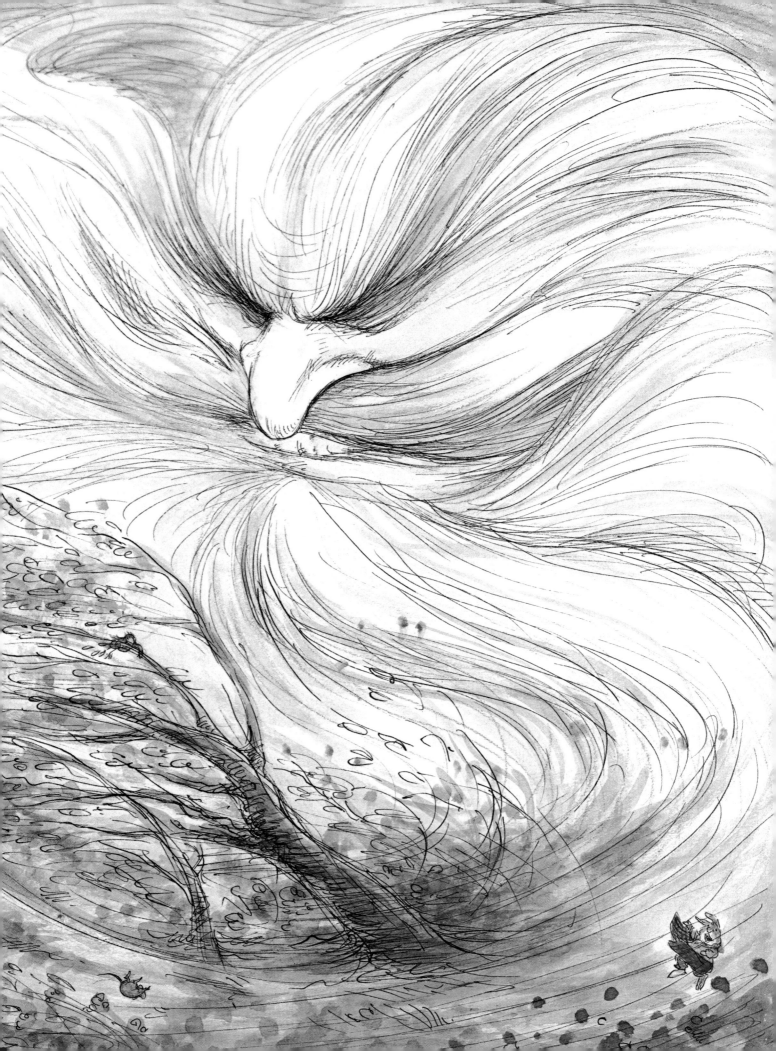

Hector Protector was dressed all in green;
Hector Protector was sent to the Queen.
The Queen did not like him,
No more did the King;
So Hector Protector was sent back again.

Darby and Joan were dressed in black,
Sword and buckle behind their back;
Foot for foot, and knee for knee,
Turn about, Darby's company.

The two gray kits,
And the gray kits' mother
All went over
The bridge together.
The bridge broke down,
They all fell in,
"May the rats go with you,"
Says Tom Bowlin.

Barber, barber, shave a pig,
How many hairs to make a wig?
Four and twenty, that's enough.
Give the barber a pinch of snuff.

As I went over the water,
The water went over me,
I saw two little blackbirds
Sitting on a tree;
One called me rascal,
The other called me thief,
I took up my little black stick
And knocked out all their teeth.

Robbin and Bobbin,
Two big-bellied men,
They ate more vittles
Than four-score and ten.

Polly put the kettle on,
Polly put the kettle on,
Polly put the kettle on,
We'll all have tea.

Sukey take it off again,
Sukey take it off again,
Sukey take it off again,
They've all gone away.

60

Charley, barley, buck and rye,
What's the way the Frenchmen fly?
Some fly east, and some fly west,
And some fly over the cuckoo's nest.

How many miles to Dover-town?
Three-score miles and ten.
Can I get there by candlelight?
Yes, and back again.

A man went a-hunting at Reigate,
And wished to leap over a high gate;
Says the owner, "Go round,
With your gun and your hound,
For you never shall jump over my gate."

There was an old woman who lived in a shoe,
She had so many children she didn't know what to do;
She gave them some broth without any bread;
She whipped them all soundly and put them to bed.

Little Jack Dandy-prat was my first suitor;
He had a dish and a spoon, and he'd some pewter;
He'd linen and woolen, and woolen and linen,
A little pig on a string cost him five shilling.

"Fire, fire!"
Said Mrs. McGuire.
"Where, where?"
Said Mrs. Ware.
"Down town!"
Said Mrs. Brown.
"Oh, Lord save us!"
Said Mrs. Davis.

63

Baby, baby, naughty baby,
Hush, you squalling thing, I say.
Peace this moment, peace, or maybe
Bonaparte will pass this way.

Baby, baby, he's a giant,
Tall and black as Rouen steeple,
And he breakfasts, dines, rely on't,
Every day on naughty people.

Baby, baby, if he hears you,
As he gallops past the house,
Limb from limb at once he'll tear you,
Just as pussy tears a mouse.

And he'll beat you, beat you, beat you,
And he'll beat you all to pap,
And he'll eat you, eat you, eat you,
Every morsel snap, snap, snap.

Here stands a fist.
Who set it there?
A better man than you,
Touch him if you dare.

Hey diddle diddle,
The cat and the fiddle,
The cow jumped over the moon;
The little dog laughed
To see such sport,
And the dish ran away with the spoon.

The fox gives warning,
It's a cold frosty morning.

If you would see a church miswent,
You must go to Cuckstone in Kent.

Some say the devil's dead,
And buried in Cold Harbor,
Others say he's rose again,
And prenticed to a barber.

To scratch where it itches
Is better than fine clothes or riches.

Jack Sprat could eat no fat,
His wife could eat no lean;
And so betwixt them both, you see,
They licked the platter clean.

Coo-oo, Coo-oo,
It's as much as a pigeon can do,
To maintain two:
But the little wren can maintain ten,
And bring them all up like gentlemen.

Taffy was a Welshman,
Taffy was a thief,
Taffy came to my house
And stole a piece of beef.

I went to Taffy's house,
Taffy wasn't in,
I jumped upon his Sunday hat
And poked it with a pin.

Taffy was a Welshman,
Taffy was a sham,
Taffy came to my house
And stole a leg of lamb.

I went to Taffy's house,
Taffy was not there,
I hung his coat and trousers
To roast before a fire.

Taffy was a Welshman,
Taffy was a cheat,
Taffy came to my house
And stole a piece of meat.

I went to Taffy's house,
Taffy was in bed,
I took a marrow bone
And flung it at his head.

The lion and the unicorn
Were fighting for the crown;
The lion beat the unicorn,
All about the town.

Some gave them white bread,
And some gave them brown;
Some gave them plum cake
And drummed them out of town.

Yankee Doodle came to town
Riding on a pony;
He stuck a feather in his hat,
And called it macaroni.

There was a man in our town,
And he was wondrous wise,
He jumped into a quickset hedge,
And scratched out both his eyes.

And when he saw his eyes were out,
With all his might and main
He jumped into another hedge,
And scratched them in again.

The man in the moon drinks claret,
But he is a dull Jack-a-dandy;
Would he know a sheep's head from a carrot
He should learn to drink cider and brandy.

There was a little guinea pig,
Who, being little, was not big,
He always walked upon his feet,
And never fasted when he eat.

When from a place he ran away,
He never at that place did stay,
And when he ran, as I am told,
He ne'er stood still for young or old.

He often squeaked and sometimes vi'lent,
And when he squeaked he ne'er was silent;
Tho ne'er instructed by a cat,
He knew a mouse was not a rat.

One day, as I am certified,
He took a whim and fairly died;
And as I'm told by men of sense,
He never has been living since.

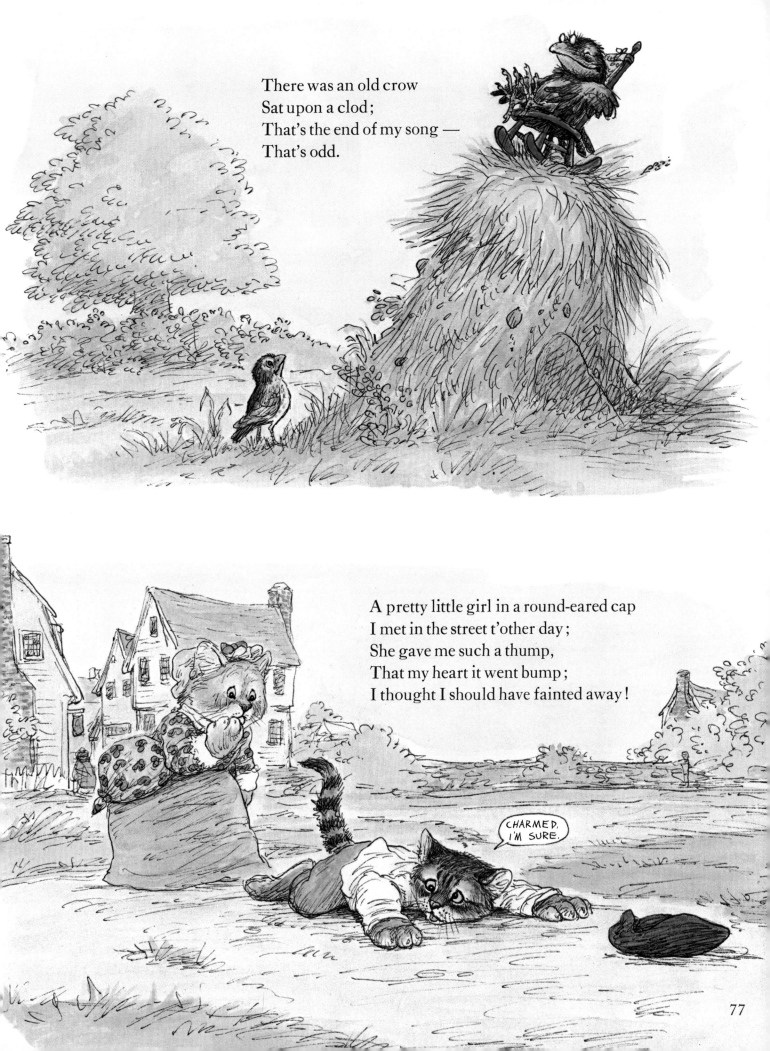

There was an old crow
Sat upon a clod;
That's the end of my song —
That's odd.

A pretty little girl in a round-eared cap
I met in the street t'other day;
She gave me such a thump,
That my heart it went bump;
I thought I should have fainted away!

CHARMED,
I'M SURE.

Terence McDiddler,
The three-stringed fiddler,
Can charm, if you please,
The fish from the seas.

A diller, a dollar,
A ten o'clock scholar,
What makes you come so soon?
You used to come at ten o'clock,
But now you come at noon.

SIR, IF I MAY BE PERMITTED TO SAY SO, SARCASM HAS NO PLACE IN THE CLASSROOM.

Bell-horses, bell-horses,
What time of day?
One o'clock, two o'clock,
Off and away!

A little pig found a fifty-dollar note,
And purchased a hat and a very fine coat,
With trousers, and stockings, and shoes,
Cravat, and shirt-collar, and gold-headed cane;
Then, proud as could be, did he march up the lane;
Says he, "I shall hear all the news."

Sing a song of sixpence,
A pocket full of rye;
Four and twenty blackbirds
Baked in a pie.

When the pie was opened
The birds began to sing;
Wasn't that a dainty dish
To set before the king?

The king was in his counting-house
Counting out his money;
The queen was in the parlor
Eating bread and honey.

The maid was in the garden
Hanging out the clothes,
When down came a blackbird
And snapped off her nose.

There was an old woman tossed in a blanket
Seventeen times as high as the moon;
What she did there, I cannot tell you,
But in her hand she carried a broom.

Old woman, old woman, old woman, said I,
Whither, oh whither, oh whither so high?
To sweep the cobwebs from the sky,
And I'll be with you by and by.

Little Polly Flinders
Sat among the cinders,
Warming her pretty little toes;
Her mother came and caught her,
And whipped her little daughter
For spoiling her nice new clothes.

I'll sing you a song,
Nine verses long,
For a pin:
Three and three are six,
And three are nine;
You are a fool,
And the pin is mine.

Jack be nimble,
Jack be quick,
Jack jump over
The candlestick.

A bag-pudding the King did make,
And stuffed it well with plums:
And in it put great lumps of fat,
As big as my two thumbs.

When good King Arthur ruled this land,
He was a goodly King;
He stole three pecks of barley-meal,
To make a bag-pudding.

The King and Queen did eat thereof,
And noblemen beside;
And what they did not eat that night
The Queen next morning fried.

J was Joe Jenkins,
Who played on the fiddle;
He began twenty times,
But left off in the middle.

The more you heap,
The worse you cheap.

Tom, Tom, the piper's son,
Stole a pig, and away he run!
The pig was eat, and Tom was beat,
And Tom went roaring down the street!

Up at Piccadilly, oh!
The coachman takes his stand,
And when he meets a pretty girl,
He takes her by the hand.
Whip away for ever, oh!
Drive away so clever, oh!
All the way to Bristol, oh!
He drives her four-in-hand.

Ride a cock-horse to Coventry Cross,
To see a fine lady upon a white horse;
Rings on her fingers and bells on her toes,
She shall have music wherever she goes.

O the little rusty dusty miller,
Dusty was his coat,
Dusty was his color,
Dusty was the kiss I got from the miller;
If I had my pockets
Full of gold and siller,
I would give it all
To my dusty miller.

There is a girl of our town,
She often wears a flowered gown:
Tommy loves her night and day,
And Richard when he may,
And Johnny when he can:
I think Sam will be the man!

Lend me your mare to ride a mile!
She's lamed, leaping over a stile.
Alack! and I must go to the fair!
I'll give you money for your mare.
Oh, oh, say you so?
Money will make the mare to go!

One to make ready,
Two to prepare,
Good luck to the rider,
And away goes the mare!

OH, OH,
BAD LUCK.

My little old man and I fell out,
How shall we bring this matter about?
Bring it about as well as you can,
Get you gone, you little old man!

Cheese and bread for gentlemen,
Hay and corn for horses,
A cup of ale for good old wives,
And kisses for young lasses.

One misty, moisty morning,
When cloudy was the weather,
There I met an old man
Clothed all in leather;
Clothed all in leather,
With cap under his chin.
How do you do, and how do you do,
And how do you do again?

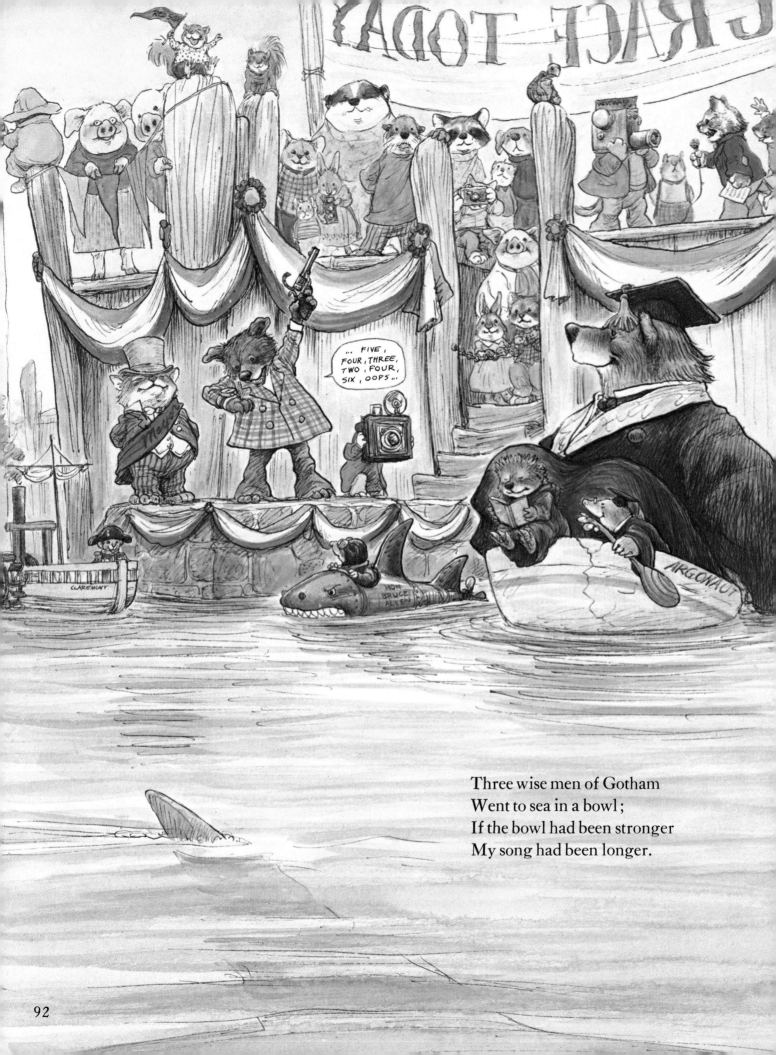

Three wise men of Gotham
Went to sea in a bowl;
If the bowl had been stronger
My song had been longer.

Rub a dub dub,
Three men in a tub,
And how do you think they got there?
The butcher, the baker,
The candlestick-maker,
They all jumped out of a rotten potato!
'Twas enough to make the fish stare.

Little Tee Wee,
He went to sea,
In an open boat;
And while afloat
The little boat bended —
My story's ended.

Two little dogs sat by the fire
Over a fender of coal-dust;
Said one little dog to the other little dog,
If you don't talk, why, I must.

It costs little Gossip her income for shoes,
To travel about and carry the news.

Tweedledum and Tweedledee
Resolved to have a battle,
For Tweedledum said Tweedledee
Had spoiled his nice new rattle.
Just then flew by a monstrous crow,
As big as a tar barrel,
Which frightened both the heroes so,
They quite forgot their quarrel.

Granfa' Grig had a pig,
In a field of clover;
Piggie died, Granfa' cried,
And all the fun was over.

Index of First Lines